MY TEACHER CAN TEACH...
ANYONE!

by W. Nikola-Lisa

illustrations by Felipe Galindo

Lee & Low Books Inc.
New York

Manufactured in China

Book design by David Neuhaus/NeuStudio
Book production by The Kids at Our House

The text is set in Hank
The illustrations are rendered in pencil, brush pen, rapidograph,
and watercolor on watercolor paper

10 9 8 7 6 5 4 3 2 1
First Edition

Library of Congress Cataloging-in-Publication Data
Nikola-Lisa, W.
My teacher can teach—anyone! / by W. Nikola-Lisa ; illustrations by Felipe Galindo.— 1st ed.
p. cm.
Summary: An alphabet story in verse about a Latino boy and his remarkable teacher who
can teach an astronaut how to float in space and instruct a ballet dancer how to land with grace.
ISBN 1-58430-163-5
1. Teachers—Fiction. 2. Occupations—Fiction. 3. Hispanic Americans—Fiction. 4. Alphabet.
5. Stories in rhyme.] I. Galindo, Felipe, ill. II. Title.
PZ8.3.N5664My 2004
[E]—dc22   2003022904

To the teacher in you, Larissa —W.N.-L.

For Andrea with love —F.G.

My teacher is so good,

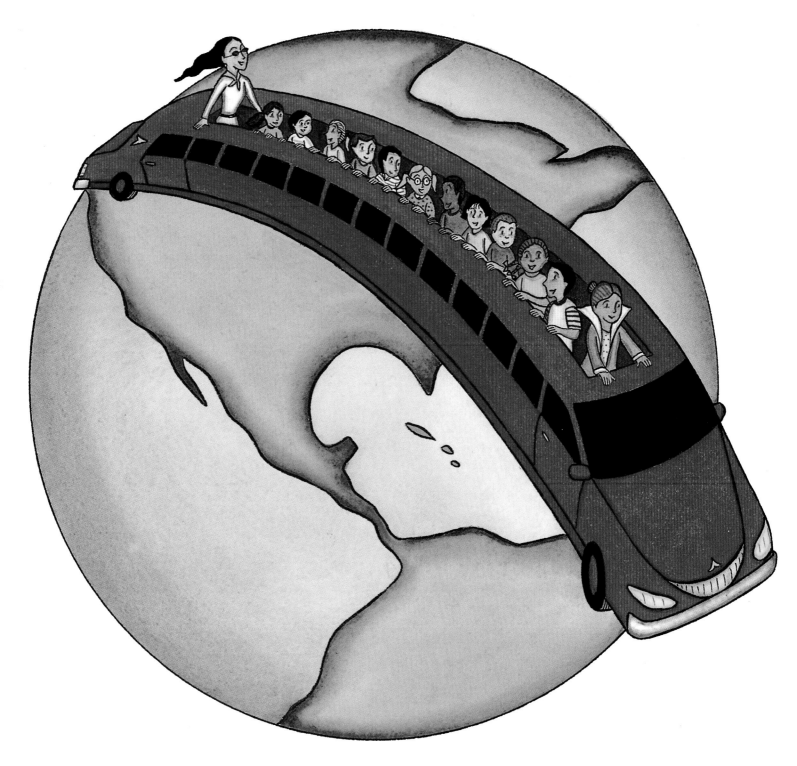

She could teach a Zillionaire
how to live in style.

she can teach . . . *anyone!*

She could teach an Astronaut
how to float in space.

She could teach a Ballet dancer
how to land with grace.

She could teach a Carpenter
how to nail a roof.

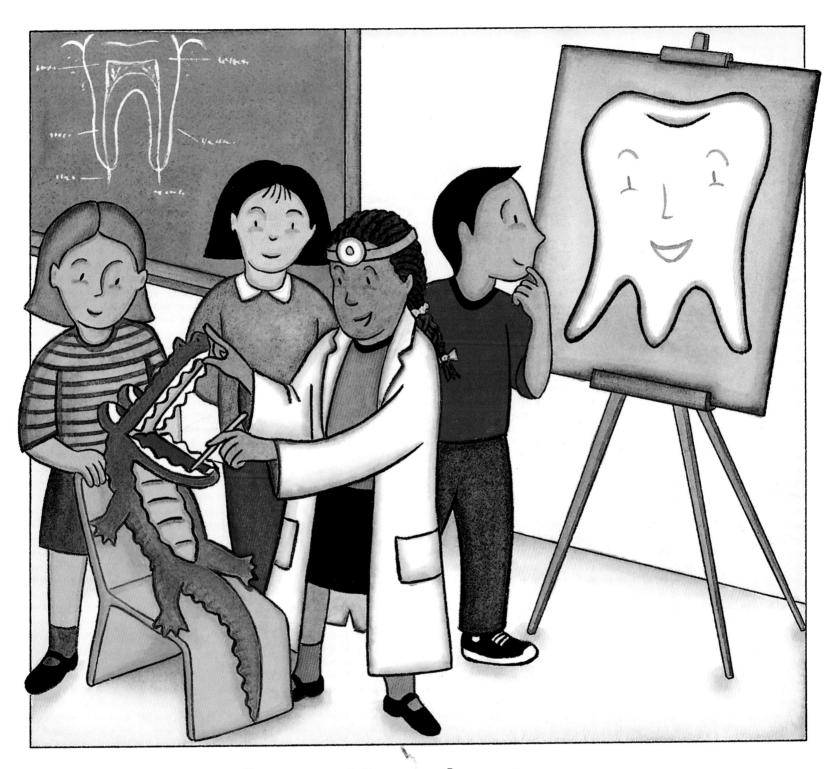

She could teach a Dentist
how to fill a tooth.

She could teach an Engineer
how to dig a hole.

She could teach a Firefighter
how to slide the pole.

She could teach the Governor
how to host a lunch.

She could teach a Heavyweight
how to throw a punch.

She could teach an Illustrator
how to draw a top.

She could teach a Janitor
how to wring a mop.

She could teach a Kayaker
how to pull a stroke.

She could teach a Logger
how to fell an oak.

She could teach a Mechanic
how to change a hose.

She could teach a Novelist
how to write in prose.

She could teach an Opera singer
how to hold a note.

She could teach the President
how to cast a vote.

She could teach a Quarterback
how to throw a ball.

She could teach a Rodeo clown
how to take a fall.

She could teach a Sailor
how to cast a jig.

She could teach a Trucker
how to drive a rig.

She could teach an Umpire
how to call an out.

She could teach a Veterinarian
how to hold a snout.

She could teach a Woodworker
how to build a trap.

She could teach a Xylophonist
how to play with snap.

She could teach a Yodeler
how to sing a mile.

Meg and her
Circus Tricks

by Graham Percy

LITTLE, BROWN AND COMPANY
Boston · Toronto · London

For Kitty

Illustrations and text copyright © 1991 by Graham Percy

First published in Great Britain in 1991 by
Little, Brown and Company (UK) Limited
Beacon House, 30 North End Road, London W14 0SH

Designed by Lisa Tai

ISBN 0-316-88864-8

A CIP catalogue record for this book
is available from the British Library

10 9 8 7 6 5 4 3 2 1

Typeset by DP Photosetting, Aylesbury, Bucks
Printed and bound in Belgium by Proost, Turnhout

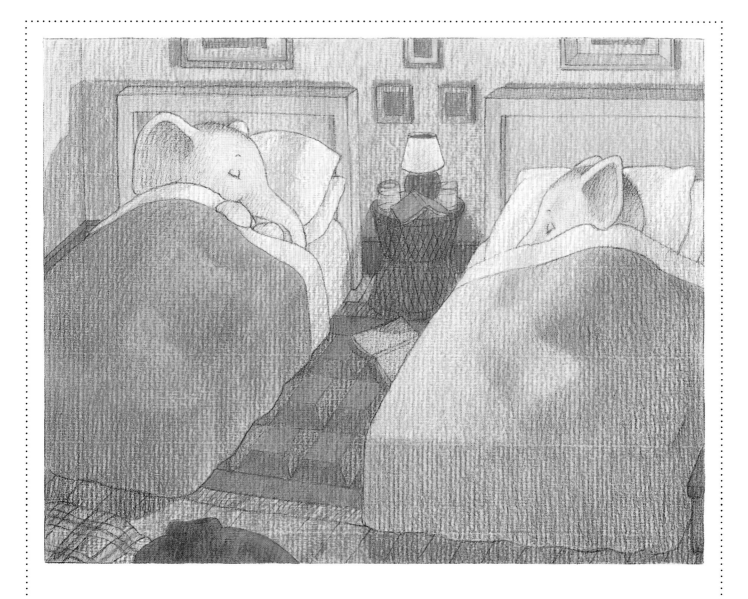

"The circus will be here tomorrow," said Max to his sister as they snuggled down in their beds. Meg shut her eyes and thought to herself, "I really love Uncle Zeb's circus."

Meg got dressed very quietly. "I wonder why Max's best clothes are all ready for him? He must have something special to do today," she thought as she closed the door.

Meg didn't have any breakfast. She rushed off down the
road towards the river. There, in the distance, she could just
see the tops of the tents and some of the trailers.

Uncle Zeb and the circus folk were lying about exhausted
from their morning work-outs. They were having tea and
pancakes and they called out ''Hello, Meg, come and join us.''

Meg was very hungry so she really enjoyed her big plate of pancakes. Then Zoltan the juggler said, "Now we'll teach you some circus tricks – first, how to do juggling!"

The Great Zoltan, as he liked to be called, showed Meg how
to practise with rolled-up socks. ''When you're learning,
wooden balls can hurt, so we start with something soft.''

Meg quickly got the idea and in no time at all she was juggling four pairs of socks without dropping a single one. Both uncle Zeb and aunt Zoey came to watch.

Now Meg heard a voice from up in a tree. It was Zelda the tightrope walker. ''Come up here Meg,'' she called down, ''and I'll show you how to do tightrope walking.''

Everyone clapped and cheered when Meg made it to the
end of the rope. Then from a nearby tent a very mysterious
voice called out, "This way Meg, to learn some real magic!"

Meg went over to the dark blue tent where the mysterious voice had come from. She peered inside and there was her uncle Zeb dressed as Count Zoff the circus magician.

"Come in my dear." His voice was like the hissing of a snake. "Get behind my magic door and I'll plunge these swords through it without harming you at all."

Eyeing the big swords nervously, Meg played for time and
said "That's a very nice cape you have there, Count Zoff."
"Yes, it was a birthday present . . ." began the Count.

But Meg didn't wait for him to finish. She dashed out of the
tent and headed straight for home. How could she have
forgotten that today was Max's birthday?

Puffing up the hill to the house, she also remembered that
her present for Max was to be a birthday party
entertainment in the garden for Max and all his friends.

She rushed into the garden and saw Max's friends. Some
were very bored and others were becoming quarrelsome.
They'd been waiting more than an hour for the show to start.

Then Meg had a bright idea. She beamed and spread her
arms out wide. "Welcome, welcome, welcome, to the
greatest show on earth," she bellowed across the lawn.

She picked up some red apples from under the tree and started juggling – first one – ''That's not difficult,'' someone said, then two, then four . . . and everyone cheered!

Now she clambered up to the heavy rope which carried
Grandpa's grapevine out over the pond. Off she went across
it, balancing with a broom . . . more clapping and cheering!

"What's next?" shouted some of Max's friends excitedly.

"The door of swords," announced Meg, and skipped off into the garage and pulled the door shut behind her.

In the dark she suddenly remembered that uncle Zeb hadn't really had time to explain how the sword trick was done. Just then, Grandma called out, "Come inside now everyone!"

"Thank goodness – saved by the birthday cake!" thought
Meg. She was just going to tell Max how she'd forgotten all
about his birthday when he bounced over and gave her a hug.

"That was amazing," he said. "You must have been working
on those tricks for weeks!" Meg started to say, "Well . . ." but
Max popped a very big piece of birthday cake into her mouth.

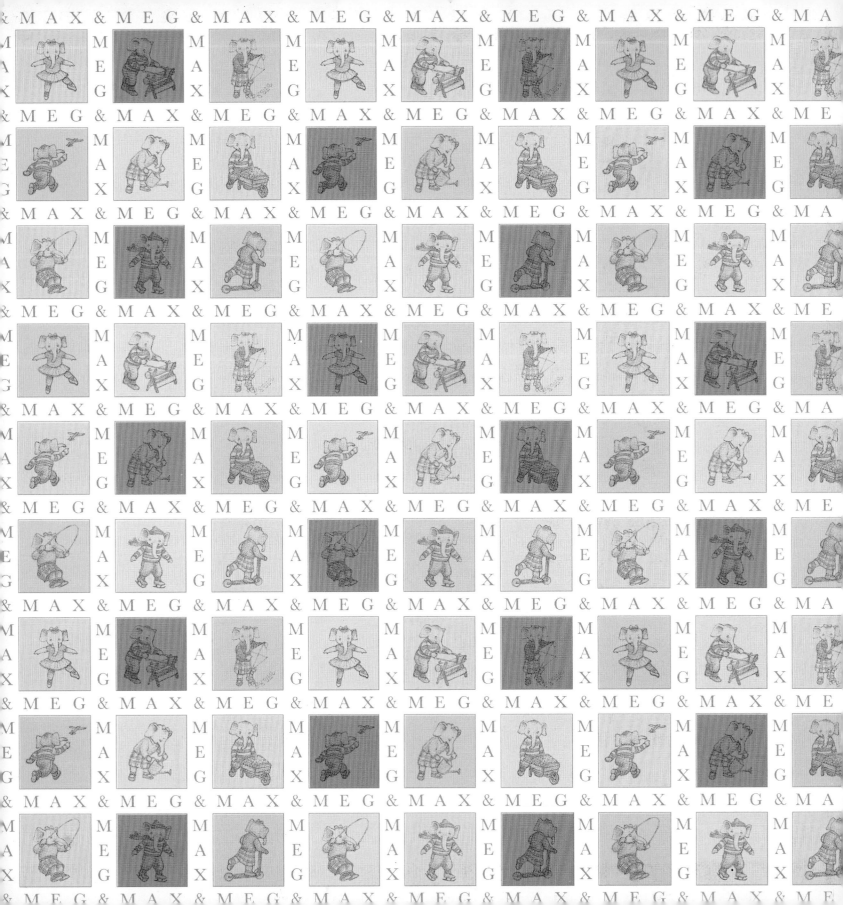